Mail Order

Hannah

Cheryl Wright

MAIL ORDER HANNAH

Copyright ©2020 by Cheryl Wright

Cover Artist: Black Widow Books

Dedication

To Margaret Tanner, my very dear friend and fellow author, for her enduring encouragement and friendship.

To Alan, my husband of over forty-eight years, who has been a relentless supporter of my writing and dreams for many years.

To Virginia McKevitt, cover artist and friend, who always creates the most amazing covers for my books.

To You, my wonderful readers, who encourage me to continue writing these stories. It is such a joy knowing so many of you enjoy reading my stories as much as I love writing them for you.

Table of Contents

Chapter One

Idaho Falls, Idaho – 1880

Hannah Wilson stared down into the crib.

Five-month-old Rosemary lay sleeping soundly. Hannah put a gentle hand to her back and felt the steady breathing of the baby.

Happy in the knowledge Rosie was alive and well, she went to the small desk tucked into the corner of the nursery.

The baby's mother had died in childbirth, and Hannah had been employed by Arthur Richardson to care for his daughter once the wet nurse had left. His business took him away from home more than he cared, and without a mother for his daughter, he was at his wit's end.

The man was often abrupt, and always in a hurry, but he did the best he could for his daughter, his only child.

Rosie stirred and Hannah returned to the crib. "It's okay, Rosie," she said quietly, laying a gentle hand on the baby's back once more.

She soon settled and Hannah went back to the desk again. She must reply to the letter in front of her. She'd already put it off for a few days, hoping her situation would change, but it wasn't to be.

Her position as Governess to young Rosie was only temporary, until Mr Richardson's cousin Melody arrived, so Hannah had put a contingency plan into effect.

Dear Mr Delbert, she wrote in her neatest copperplate handwriting.

Thank you for your latest correspondence. I feel we are quite compatible going by the several letters we've had back and forth. Since you are still willing, I would be more than pleased to enter into a marriage with you.

My employer, Mr Richardson, is about to leave to fetch his cousin after her long trip from London. She's the one who will provide permanent care for Rosie. He is due back in about three weeks, at which time I will be free to travel to Grand Falls.

Thank you for the train ticket and the notes to pay for my expenses along the way. You have been more than generous.

By my reckoning, I should arrive at Grand Falls on the twenty-first of next month.

Kindest regards,

Miss Hannah Wilson

She read over the letter again, ensuring it made sense. Convinced it did, she stood and stretched. She'd agonized over this decision – never in her wildest dreams did Hannah believe she would ever become a mail order bride.

Having limited employment options, she had little choice. The worst of it all being she would miss little Rosie as she'd grown very attached to her. But Hannah knew having family care for the child was the best option for her.

Hannah had only secured the position due to knowing Mr Richardson through their mutual church. When Ethel Richardson had died giving little Rosemary life, it was a great tragedy, but it left her father in a bind.

How could he run his business with a newborn to care for? The short answer was he couldn't.

At first he was able to secure a wet nurse, but she was only available for two months, then would again leave Rosie without anyone to care for her.

Because she was the only unattached female available at the time, Mr Richardson approached Hannah to care for the child.

Of course there was the question of improprieties. Hannah could not stay in his house without a chaperone, so Mr Richardson had secured his elderly cousin to live with them until cousin Melody arrived, and Hannah left to be married.

Despite the success of his business, Mr Richardson didn't pay well – far from it. She received free room and board, plus a small stipend. For that she was expected to provide around the clock care for Rosie.

Not that she needed a lot of money – her main expense was clothing; she had no time for socializing and therefore had no friends.

She shrugged. She'd had no other options or opportunities at the time, so she'd decided to take up his less than generous offer. With their arrangement ending soon, she had to prepare for the inevitable.

There was a time when Hannah had hoped Mr Richardson would change his mind and keep her on. But it wasn't to be. His cousin had written a few months ago and confirmed her passage from England. She had even stated a time to be collected from the port which was a good six days ride away by carriage.

Hannah pulled the curtains aside and stared at the scene before her. Rolling hills and green pastures – she would miss this place. She'd been brought up here in Idaho Falls after her parents had been killed in an accident many years ago.

Her grandparents had taken her in, but they were long gone and now she was completely alone. She had little in the way of employable skills, but she was certainly good at looking after children. It was her main attribute and what had kept her employed, albeit periodic.

The door suddenly flew open and Mr Richardson stood in the doorway, motioning for her to come out.

She gently closed the door behind her, not wanting to wake the baby.

"I'm leaving now," he said in a whisper. "I'll be gone for about three weeks." He reached into his pocket and pulled out a wad of money. "Take this, and buy any supplies you need."

Hannah's eyes opened wide. It was more money than she'd ever seen before. "That's far too much, Mr Richardson," she said, reluctant to take such a large sum despite him being such a miser in the past.

He shook his head. "You will need to buy food and milk for the baby, as well as anything else you require while I'm gone." He pushed the notes into her hands. "I'll feel more comfortable knowing you can deal with any situation that might occur in my absence."

In that case... "Thank you, Mr Richardson." She glanced over the landing and saw his suitcases sitting at the front door. "Oh, I've told Mr Delbert I shall arrive at my destination on the twenty-first. Does that sound feasible to you?"

The last thing she wanted to do was let him down, even if he did pay her a pittance. Besides, Rosie was her priority.

He seemed thoughtful for long moments. Probably working out dates in his head Hannah decided. "Yes. Yes, the twenty-first is very doable." He opened the door and strolled over to the crib where he stared down at his sleeping daughter. He blew a kiss so as not to wake her. "I love you Rosemary," he whispered, then left the room again.

"I will see you in a few weeks," he told Hannah, then disappeared down the stairs.

Grand Falls

"Put my purchases on my account, will you?" Mrs Thompson said as she placed her shopping on the counter.

Cecil Delbert nodded. "Of course. What do you have planned for today," he asked, although he wasn't really interested. He wrote each item in the account book, then added the purchases to a large brown bag.

"Thank you, Mrs Thompson," he said, carrying her shopping and holding the door open for her. "I'll see you next time." He handed the large bag over, then closed the door behind her.

When he first opened the store, he could easily manage on his own. But now it had become far too large for one person to run alone. The Mercantile was always busy, being the only large store for many miles around. It was the main reason he'd decided to send for a mail order bride.

He reached into his apron pocket and retrieved the latest letter Miss Wilson had sent. She had the most beautiful handwriting, and that would bode well when she filled out the account book.

On the one occasion he'd employed someone to help out in the store, their writing was appalling. He couldn't read a word, and as it turned out, neither could they.

It had cost him dearly.

Since he couldn't interpret the entries, he couldn't charge the customers. It was a huge blow to his profits. He vowed never to employ a clerk again.

But a mail order bride? That was different. She would benefit from the correct entry of all purchases, with their profits helping both herself and him.

They had sent several letters back and forth, and Miss Wilson had sent him a photograph. While he may not call her stunningly beautiful, she certainly wasn't hard to look at.

He stared at the writing on the envelope. He could stand here all day and not open it. Cecil knew he was acting childishly. This letter would either be an acceptance, or a rejection of his offer of marriage.

He'd purchased tickets for her in the hope she accepted, and added what he believed would be enough money and then some, to ensure she was well-fed and accommodated on the trip here.

She would travel by train, then change lines for another far shorter leg on another train. It would be rather arduous, but he hoped it was well worth it for his potential bride.

That was if she didn't turn him down. He'd heard of mail order brides who took the pre-purchased tickets and cashed them in, as well as pocketing the money.

He didn't have any inkling Miss Wilson was like that.

Chapter Two

Hannah's suitcase was packed. She didn't possess a lot of belongings – a few changes of clothes, a nightgown and undergarments, and an extra pair of shoes.

She had placed a complete change of clothes in her carpetbag, since there was to be an overnight stay before she boarded the train on the second train line. It would be a blessed relief too.

Not that she'd ever ridden a train herself, but she'd heard horror stories of how unpleasant it could be. A night in a hotel in a comfortable bed would bode well for the remainder of her trip.

Little Rosie began to cry, and Hannah removed the baby from her crib. She gave her a warm bath, then changed her into a dry diaper and dressed her in clean clothes. Finally, she wrapped her in a clean blanket.

Once she was finished, Rosie was well ready to be fed. She stretched her tiny arms and legs and let out a yawn. Then her pink tongue darted out of her mouth like it always did when she was hungry.

Hannah placed her back in the crib while she prepared her bottle.

Lifting Rosie out of the crib to feed her, she lamented the impending loss of the small child in her arms. She had become very fond of this little human, more than she ever imagined she could.

Mr Richardson was due back in two days, and then she would leave Rosie in the care of cousin Melody who was to become the second Mrs Richardson.

Hannah could only assume the baby would be in safe hands. The child's father surely wouldn't bring someone all the way across the world without checking her credentials, even if they were related.

Despite being cold and distant toward her, he was always warm and happy around his daughter. She was all he had – she knew this because he'd told her often enough. She'd wondered if it was his way of justifying the diminutive wage he paid her.

Melody was a distant cousin and even then, he'd had trouble locating her. She just hoped Mr Richardson knew what he was doing – after all, his daughter's life would be in this woman's hands.

She had just begun to feed the baby when there was urgent pounding on the door. Not just knocking, but pounding and yelling.

Hannah heard the front door open, then the noise ceased. She breathed a sigh of relief.

"Miss Wilson," she heard the shouting as Mr Richardson's elderly cousin twice removed partially climbed the stairs to the nursery. "Miss Wilson,

Hannah," she said again, only far more breathless this time. "It's the police!"

She turned to see the elderly widow white as a ghost, and more than a little worried.

Not wishing to disturb the content baby, she carried her down the stairs in her arms to greet their odd visitor.

"Good afternoon, Ma'am," the officer greeted her.

"Good afternoon, Officer," she said warily. "I am Miss Hannah Wilson – Rosemary's Governess."

His brow furrowed and he looked even more worried than previously. "Is there somewhere we can sit down and talk?" He looked down at Rosie and his face softened.

They moved into the sitting room, Hannah even more concerned than before. As she sat, she put a cloth to her shoulder and began to pat the child's back. Not a word had been spoken.

Her heart pounded in her chest. The longer he sat silently, the more concerned she became. "Is everything okay?" she finally blurted out, almost at the same time the baby burped.

"Can you hand the baby to the housekeeper?" he asked. "I really need to speak to you uninterrupted.

The widow harrumphed. "I am no housekeeper," she said gruffly. "I am here because of the improprieties of Miss Wilson and Mr Richardson being alone in this house."

Hannah did her best to contain her mirth. The old lady hated being here, and was anxiously awaiting Hannah's departure so she could return home.

The officer glanced at Hannah.

"Well get on with it," he was told gruffly. "I don't have all day."

That's exactly what the old lady did have. Hannah did everything around the house, as well as taking care of the baby. She even cooked the meals.

Hannah's heart-rate quickened. Whatever could be wrong? "Please get this over with. I am feeling quite concerned by your visit. Besides, I need to attend to the baby."

"Very well. There's been an accident. Mr Richardson and his companion are both dead."

"Dead?" She suddenly felt light-headed. She had heard wrong. They couldn't be dead – what was to happen to Rosie? She couldn't bear the thought the child would end up in an orphanage.

Tears welled in her eyes.

"I'm sorry to be the bearer of bad news, Miss Wilson." He stood and headed toward the front door.

"Dead?" the old lady screeched. "That's it, I'm out of here. Finally, I can go home." She was up and headed toward her room, presumably to pack. She stopped momentarily and addressed the officer. "I ain't taking no kid either. I'm too old." She scurried out of the room before another word could be said.

Hannah's brain was in a fog, and she continued to sit, trying to take it all in. "Wait!" she finally called after him, his hand on the door handle. The officer turned back. "What am I meant to do about the baby?" She stood then, confused and unsure about her immediate future. "I, I'm leaving here in two days to get married. There is no family to take Rosie. Please don't make me take her to an orphanage."

"Baby?" he said with a wink. "I don't see any baby." He moved closer and whispered conspiratorially. "Take her with you, or that's exactly where she'll end up. I have children, Miss Wilson, I'd hate to see that child in one of those hell-holes."

Take her?

"Mr Richardson obviously trusted you with his daughter, or he would not have left her with you."

He was right – Mr Richardson did trust her. He'd left Rosie with her for the past almost three weeks. But what was she to do now? In only two days she was to leave here and travel to Grand Falls to be married.

Still in shock, Hannah scribbled off a quick letter to Mr Delbert the next morning.

Dear Mr Delbert,

The situation has suddenly changed, and I must bring my young charge with me. Mr Richardson and his cousin were killed in a tragic accident, and Rosemary has no-one to care for her.

Therefore she will accompany me to Grand Falls. I hope this change of plans meets with your approval. If not, please advise at your earliest convenience.

Kindest regards,

Miss Hannah Wilson

She wrote the address and placed Rosie in her carriage. They would take a stroll down to the post office and post the letter.

Surely Mr Delbert wouldn't refuse a small orphan child?

She shook herself. He seemed like such a caring man, not the kind to turn a baby away. What she would do if that possibility did occur, Hannah had no idea.

At the very least, she would find a boarding house to stay in until more firm arrangements could be made. At the worst, she would return home where she would have the support of her church family.

The weather was fine, and the fresh air would do them both good. Hannah had to admit it was the one thing she didn't do often enough, and that was take the young girl for regular walks.

She opened her reticule to locate a stamp, only to come across the wad of money Mr Richardson had given her. She gasped. It had totally slipped her mind.

What was she meant to do with all that money? It wasn't hers to keep, but on the other hand, she may need it to set Rosie up at their destination.

She couldn't take much with her – the carriage of course, her clothes and diapers, blankets, as well as her bottles and some toys.

Apart from that, she would have to leave everything else behind. She couldn't even take the crib. There would be no way to manage all that, along with her own belongings on two trains.

If she didn't have so much to do before leaving here, Hannah would have sat down and had a good cry. Get her distress out of her system.

They began their stroll to the post office, and Rosie slept most of the way. Mr Richardson lived a little way out of town, but not so far she couldn't walk there.

When they finally arrived, she handed over her correspondence. "How long will it take to get there?" she asked the postmaster.

He scrutinized the address. "It could be a day or a month," he said nonchalantly.

"A month!" It had to get their sooner. Mr Delbert needed to know before her arrival.

"Sorry Miss," he said. "Look on the bright side, it might arrive by the end of the week."

She prayed for the best case scenario.

Hannah left the post office feeling more than a little despondent. She didn't want any surprises for her potential groom when she arrived in Grand Falls.

Everything had been carefully planned – they'd been writing to each other for some months, and had seemed to be compatible. There had not been mention of children, but she'd assumed that would be something for their future.

What Cecil Delbert would think of her bringing this little surprise package with her, goodness only knew.

She decided to return home a different way, a more scenic way, since this was the last time she would venture out here. She spotted a wooden seat in a park not far from town.

Hannah sat down and breathed in the brisk afternoon air. She checked in the carriage to find Rosie still sound asleep, so closed her eyes and began to pray.

She'd done a lot of praying over the past two days – including prayer for the soul of Mr Richardson and his cousin who had been taken far too soon.

She also prayed Rosie would be accepted by Cecil Delbert and the people of Grand Falls. Then she prayed for their future.

When she opened her eyes, Hannah felt far better. She could have done her praying at the church, but it was on the other side of town, and she had a lot to do before departing for her new home.

Feeling as though a weight had been lifted from her shoulders, she began the trek home again.

Such a tragedy for poor Rosie. First her mother, then her father. Hannah felt as though the loss was hers to bear. The sooner they got away from Idaho Falls the better in her opinion.

The circumstances of the past two days were starting to get to her.

"Please stop crying Rosie." Hannah patted the baby's back. They'd survived the first leg of the train trip without too much hassle, but now she wouldn't stop crying.

Hannah was sure there would be complaints from the other hotel guests. It wasn't like Rosie to cry like this – she was such a good baby. She'd been fed, her diaper changed, and she'd even had a warm bath.

Laying the baby down, she checked her diaper again. It was dry. What on earth was wrong with her?

She would take her for a walk except it was dark outside. Besides they were in a strange place, and she had no idea how safe it was.

Perhaps they could stroll up and down the corridors. She wrapped Rosie tightly in her blankets, she seemed to like being tightly wrapped, then placed her back in her carriage. She rocked the carriage slightly and she began to settle.

It seemed she'd become used to the rocking on the rickety train. Hannah had found herself drifting off on more than one occasion and had forced herself to stay awake. She wasn't going to risk someone either taking Rosie, or her reticule with Mr Richardson's money.

She decided since it was becoming dark, it must be near supper time. Then it hit her, perhaps she was hungry for solid food. Hannah was so stressed over the events of the past few days she wasn't thinking straight.

She continued to rock the carriage and headed for the dining room of the hotel. She just hoped the prices weren't out of her reach – that money was for the necessities, not for her to indulge in a high-priced meal.

The dining room was near empty by the time she arrived there. A waitress, who said her name was Mary, came over and handed her a menu. "I'm sorry Miss, but we're almost out of food. I can give you a hearty beef soup with a bread roll if that will help quell your hunger."

She looked apologetic, and Hannah felt sorry for her. "Thank you, that sounds lovely," she said graciously. After their trip and all that rocking, she didn't feel like much anyway. In fact she felt rather squeamish. Hopefully food would help to settle her stomach down.

"I have some stewed fruit if you'd like it for the little one?" She glanced at the baby in the carriage. "It's on the house. She won't eat much."

"Oh no," Hannah said, I couldn't do that. I'll pay." The waitress shrugged and returned to the kitchen.

Hannah had enough money to pay her way, and would ensure she did. The hotel was not overly expensive, not to her mind anyway, and the money Cecil Delbert had sent her had proven to be far more than she needed for the trip.

The woman soon returned with the food. Almost at the same time, Rosie began to cry again. She rocked the carriage, but it didn't work this time.

"Eat your food," Mary said. "I'll look after your baby." By this time, the dining room was empty.

She lifted Rosie from the carriage and began to feed her from a small spoon. She immediately stopped crying. It was a blessed relief. The past few days had been more than a little trying.

Chapter Three

"You look frazzled, Cecil," Joe Hartley, the town tailor, told him.

Cecil looked about the store, then leaned in. "My bride is arriving later today."

Joe stepped back. "Bride? You're getting married?" He slapped Cecil on the back. "Congratulations! Getting married was the best thing I ever did."

Cecil dug into his pocket and pulled out a photograph, handing it over to Joe. "She's pretty enough," he said quietly.

"What's wrong with you? She's beautiful!"

"I guess." He picked up a broom and began to sweep out the store. "Can't have her coming here to a messy store," he said, a grin on his face.

"Well, congratulations again," Joe said. "I'd better get back to it."

Cecil looked down at his pocket-watch. Only an hour and she would be here. He'd already made arrangements with Pastor Devon so they could be married before the end of the day.

He was too nervous to do much of anything, so Cecil wandered around the store and inspected the shelves. He wiped down anything that was dusty, straightened products that were out of place, and fixed price tags that were falling off. He also filled shelves that were almost empty, bringing boxes out from the storeroom.

He couldn't remember having been so anxious before.

He checked his pocket-watch again. Only fifteen minutes until the train was due to arrive.

Was he still presentable? Did he need to wash up after cleaning down the shelves? He really wasn't sure, so instead of taking a chance, he put up the closed sign and went out the back to the residence.

He went straight to the bathroom and stared at himself in the mirror. The first thing he noticed was the apron that still hung around his neck.

It was gone in an instant.

He gazed at his reflection then washed his face with a cloth. He'd been covered in dust. Cecil combed his hair and dusted down his white shirt, put on a tie, then added a jacket over the top.

Now he was ready to meet his new bride.

He snatched up the apron he'd earlier discarded, then headed to the kitchen to retrieve the bouquet of flowers he'd arranged for her. He didn't like the thought of arriving at the train station with nothing for her, and flowers would be a nice touch.

At least Cecil thought so.

He wrapped the flowers as best he could with the tops of the flowers still showing, took a deep breath, then let himself out the main door of the residence.

The train station wasn't far from town, and he was able to stroll there in less than ten minutes. He received a few strange looks from the towns folk, mostly those who knew he would normally be in the store at this time of day.

He was certain at least some of them wondered about the flowers too.

Entering the large pavilion leading onto the platform, the smell of soot offended his senses. He could only wonder how Hannah Wilson must be feeling. She would be surrounded by this offensive odor.

He'd been there just a few minutes when he heard the train whistle blast. It wasn't far away. His heart thudded. Soon he would be a married man.

A small crowd waited on the platform, and most of them moved forward in anticipation. Cecil moved closer too.

It was all hustle and bustle on the platform now with porters bringing trolleys full of luggage, conductors helping women down the steps, and gents helping their wives with baby carriages.

Children were running from one end of the platform and being admonished by the conductor. This was no place for games – it was far too dangerous for that.

And then he spotted her. Joe Harkley was right – she was a beauty. Even after such a long and arduous trip, she looked the picture of perfection.

He watched as she instructed the porter to place her luggage on a trolley, then made his way toward her.

"Miss Hannah Wilson? I am Cecil Delbert," he said, his heartrate betraying his outward demeanor.

She glanced up at him. "Good to finally meet you," she said, but she looked harried and anxious. "I, I…"

He handed her the flowers and she blushed. "Thank you." She looked even prettier with her cheeks so pink.

"I'll take care of your luggage," he said, and handed the porter a small tip.

"Good," she said quickly. "You got my letter about Rosie."

Now he was confused. "Letter? Rosie? Is this the letter to say you were coming? I did get it, that's why I'm here now."

She stepped aside and the baby carriage was in full view. His eyes opened wide. *What sort of tomfoolery was this?*

"I didn't agree to a baby!" he almost shouted. How dare she spring a baby on him? There had been plenty of time to tell him about the child but she had cleverly omitted that fact.

"I can explain," she said, obviously distressed. She blinked trying to fight back tears, and she turned her face away.

He was angry. Beyond furious. This was not what he'd agreed to. Was this another one of those tricks he'd heard some mail order brides pulled on unwitting grooms?

"I sent an additional letter – a few days ago, when I found out."

His hands fisted by his sides and his spine stiffened Cecil was ready to walk away. He turned in his fury and began to go back the way he came. "I got no letter," he said over his shoulder.

"Mr Delbert," she shouted after him. "The baby is not mine."

Not hers? "You expect me to believe that?" What would she come up with next?

"You have to believe me. Both her parents are dead."

Dead? Both of them? That was a little hard to swallow.

He stared into her face. She was exhausted, and now he'd verbally attacked her and caused her distress.

It gave him reason to pause and think.

She'd traveled for several days to get here – surely she wouldn't have done that if she set out to deceive him. She would have taken his money and run.

The baby began to cry, and distressed herself, Hannah leaned down and picked her up. "She's hungry," she said. "And she's wet."

He got a glimpse of the baby – she looked to be a sweet thing.

She pleaded with her eyes for him to listen. "I'll just change her over there on the bench seat," she said.

"No!" he said urgently. "You can't do that out in public." *What would people think? That he had fathered this child? And now the mother had run to him?*

He scrubbed his hands through his hair.

He was still angry, but now he'd got a glimpse of the tiny cherub he wasn't sure what to do. "We'll go back to my place where you can change her. Then I'm putting you back on the train."

He watched as she straightened her shoulders and stiffened her back. "If that is what you wish," she said. "But I am not leaving today. Or even tomorrow. I've spent the last few days traveling, and I've had enough."

She had backbone, Cecil would give her that.

He nodded and they headed toward his store.

Now that Rosie was changed, she settled a little, but she was hungry. Cecil Delbert looked impatient, not to mention annoyed. Hannah couldn't blame him.

The carriage sat in a corner of the room, but she held Rosie in her arms. Perhaps if he saw her properly, and understood what a good baby she was, he wouldn't be so irate.

"It all happened so quickly," she said quietly. "One minute I was waiting for her father and his cousin to return so I could leave to come here, and then..." She felt like she would burst into tears at any moment. That was the last thing Hannah wanted.

She swallowed – hard. "And then the police were on the doorstep telling me Mr Richardson and his cousin were dead and I had to bring Rosie with me or they'd put her in an orphanage."

"An orphanage? You can't be serious?"

"There is no family to take her in." Rosie hiccupped and Hannah put the baby to her shoulder and patted her back. She was hungry and needed to be fed.

"Do you have any stewed fruit or vegetables? Or even some bread and milk?"

He jumped up from his chair. "I have some stewed apple. Would that do?"

Finally, some good news.

She'd begun to panic, but now that *his* anxiety had subsided, she felt calmer. "Here, can you hold her while I sort out her food?" Instead of waiting for an answer, she handed him the baby and left the room.

This was going to be far harder than Hannah had ever imagined.

Cecil stared down at the baby in his arms.

How did it come to this? One minute he was prepared to marry a young spinster, and next he was being asked to become a father with an instant family.

He shook his head. It wasn't going to happen. The moment the child was fed, he would ship them over to the hotel, and in a couple of days would be rid of the pair of them when the train left Grand Falls.

He turned toward the kitchen. Cecil could hear Hannah, Miss Wilson, fixing the baby's food. He was startled when tiny fingers reached up and patted his cheek.

Glancing down was the worst thing he could have done. She was smiling at him.

He didn't need this – he was a businessman with the need for someone to help out in his store. His request most certainly did not include a child, especially one this small that would require constant attention.

He opened his mouth to call Miss Wilson, to ask her to hurry up. The moment he did, tiny fingers reached into his mouth and held tight to his teeth.

Cecil tried to pull his eyes away from the tiny creature he'd had forced on him, but it wasn't happening. Her big brown eyes shone and she giggled at him.

"You really are quite sweet, aren't you?"

"She really is," Hannah said, watching him from the doorway.

He turned toward her, embarrassed at allowing himself to be taken in by the giggling child. "Ow! That hurt!" He reached up to released her fingers from his slightly too long hair, but she had a firm grip.

Hannah laughed. "That's one of her favorite things to do," she said. "Apart from snatching spectacles, that is."

She looked even more beautiful when she laughed. It was the first time he'd seen her so much as smile. Previously she'd been far too distressed to do anything but scowl.

It was more than obvious to Cecil that she would make an excellent mother for any children they might have.

Not knowing where that thought came from, he inwardly shook himself.

She sat opposite him and pulled out a clean diaper to put on the baby's front, ready to feed her.

He began to hand her back. "Would you mind?" she asked. "It would be far easier if you hold her."

What could he say? That he wouldn't do this small thing to help her out? "Of course not."

Little did he know more food would end up on him and his floor than in Rosie's mouth. "What's her name?"

She glanced at him curiously. "Rosie. Didn't I tell you that?"

"Her real name, I mean? Is it Rose?" He had no idea why he had even asked. In two days they would be gone from here, and he'd still be single and running the store alone.

"Rosemary. Her full name is Rosemary. Her father called her Rosie for short." She swallowed and a sadness crossed her face.

"Did you know him well? Her father I mean?" He really knew nothing of the father, and very little of his demise. And what of the mother?

"I have acted as temporary Governess for Rosie for the past few months, but I knew the family from our mutual church." She put another spoonful of stewed apple in the baby's mouth. "Her mother died in childbirth, and Mr Richardson, Rosie's father, arranged for a wet nurse who took care of her for the first two months."

She wiped the baby's face, then cleaned up her hands as best she could without a wet cloth. "I was brought in for the three months until Mr Richardson's cousin could take over. Now they're both dead, and Rosie has no family. No one who cares about her."

She looked distraught again. He could imagine the past days must have been quite traumatic.

"Except you," he said. "It's very obvious you care about her."

"Yes, I do," she said quietly. "How could anyone not care for her?"

She suddenly changed the subject. "Can you hold her again while I wet this face cloth? I won't be long." She left the room before he could answer, and Rosie pulled at his hair again, making Cecil wish he'd been to the barber as he'd planned.

His hands closed over hers, trying to free his hands. Her skin was so soft, and her hands so tiny.

Then she stared at him and giggled. How anyone could resist that sweet face he would never know. How *he* was going to resist *her* was more the question. It begged the question – did Hannah Wilson purposely leave him with the child so he would take a liking to her?

He thought not.

She soon returned with the wet cloth and cleaned Rosie up properly. "That's much better," he said, finally over the shock of their first meeting, and feeling a little more connected to the whole scenario.

"I'll just clean up this mess, and then I'll be back for her." She picked up the bowl with the remaining apples. "If you don't mind that is?"

He nodded. The best thing for them all would be if they left sooner rather than later. It was such a pity as he was warming to Miss Wilson.

Rosie snuggled into him, and reached her hands up to his cheeks, rubbing her fingers along his chin. "Pa-pa."

His heart thudded in his chest. *She thought he was her father?* His heart broke for the dear little orphan sitting on his knee.

What would his sister say if he sent this child away? Not to mention rejecting his bride-to-be?

Forget his sister, what would Mrs Baker from the Diner say? She would have a real time of it, making sure he knew about her distaste at his callous behavior.

Before he knew what was happening, she pulled herself up on her knees and held him by his cheeks. "Pa-pa." She moved in quickly and gave him a big sloppy kiss, her arms now wrapped around his neck.

What sort of person was he to send these two away? He wondered where would they end up if he reneged on his agreement.

The way his thoughts went did not paint a nice picture.

"Is everything alright here?"

He wondered how long she had stood in his doorway watching the antics of this dear child. "Everything is perfectly fine."

Rosie moved in for a hug, a big grin on her face. "Papa," she said again, and he was almost beginning to believe it.

"I've been thinking," he began. Cecil wasn't sure if he was in his right mind, or whether he'd been manipulated by two very clever females.

Chapter Four

Cecil waited out in the kitchen with Rosie while Hannah changed her clothes and freshened up.

If they were going to do this, she was going to look presentable. She pulled her best gown out of the trunk, and began to change.

She washed her face and hands, then brushed out her hair and pulled it into a chignon. Then she pulled on her best bonnet. Not that she had many. The money she'd made from Mr Richardson was barely enough for necessities. It certainly didn't buy luxury items like new bonnets.

"Are you ready yet, Miss Wilson?" Her groom-to-be called through the door.

She opened the door, and there he stood. "Ah, Miss Wilson. Does Rosie require any attention?"

As it happened, she didn't. Hannah had already changed her, and dressed her in fresh clothes. "Don't you think it's time you called me Hannah? The preacher will think it rather strange if you address me as Miss Wilson."

She knew she was right. More to the point, what would the preacher say about Rosie? That was going to be the test.

"Shall we go," he asked, straightening his tie.

"We shall." She grinned. He was obviously nervous, but she was nervous too. Never in a million years did she imagine herself becoming mother to an orphaned baby. Nor did she imagine she would be getting married to a complete stranger.

She didn't feel desperate, but desperation had led her to register as mail order bride. She had no plans and no prospects after her arranged time looking after Rosie. She certainly didn't want to end up homeless.

Although the pastor's wife back home had ensured her that wouldn't happen. If it came to that, she had promised to take Hannah on as governess to her own children. Hannah knew she was saying it because she felt sorry for her.

They left the residence and headed toward the church, hidden at the back of the main street. The town looked to be nice – friendly – and there were a variety of businesses here.

She pushed the carriage and was enjoying the sunshine and fresh air. She was certain Rosie would be too. They had both endured far more soot-filled days than she cared to remember.

They came to some steps at the end of the boardwalk, and Cecil lifted the carriage down. "It's just around the corner now," he said.

Just as well, because Hannah was feeling more than a little anxious now.

They turned the corner and she stopped, taking in the scene before her. "It's beautiful," she said, staring at the building. "It's far bigger than my church back home."

He went ahead and opened the carved door for her, and waited for her to push Rosie through the door. "This is lovely, Cecil," she said, glancing about.

Rosie was visually exploring her new surroundings.

"Wait," he suddenly said. She stared at him. Had he changed his mind? "Before we go in, I want to clarify this is to be a marriage of convenience."

"You don't want children?" she asked shocked. "Heirs?"

He turned to face her. "We have Rosie."

She nodded. "I understand," she said quietly, but not really comprehending why he would make such a decision.

He continued to hold the door open while they moved toward the front where the preacher waited patiently for them.

The ceremony hadn't taken as long as Hannah thought it would.

In less then fifteen minutes her life had changed forever. Whether that would be for the better, she wasn't sure yet.

"We have to get back and re-open the Mercantile," Cecil announced as they left the church.

"Of course." It might not have been the wedding she'd dreamed of as a little girl, but now she was a wife and mother. A few days ago she was neither.

Back then she was the Governess to this sweet little girl, and planning her life as the Mercantile owner's wife.

She dreamed of their future children, and the way their lives would be intertwined.

A marriage of convenience was not in her plans. Or her dreams.

When they arrived back at the residence, Cecil unlocked the door and picked her up. "Wait," she said quietly. "You're carrying me across the threshold?"

He hesitated. "You don't want me to?"

She did, she really did. But he wanted a marriage of convenience and she didn't. Especially after being this close to him. Hannah breathed in and the essence of Cecil hit her senses. Her arms slid up around his neck, and she became more aware of their closeness than she had just moments ago.

She smiled. "Yes, I do." She sighed then, and rested her head against his shoulder. She could stay like this forever.

"Pa-pa."

They both glanced back at Rosie. She was becoming impatient.

Cecil stepped forward and deposited Hannah on the floor without further interaction. He then rolled the carriage inside and the moment was gone.

Closing the door he glanced at his pocket-watch. "Goodness me," he said urgently. "It is far later than I'd anticipated. I must re-open the Mercantile. My customers will be frustrated at the delay."

"I'll organize your luncheon. Would you like me to bring it in when it's ready?"

He turned to her. "That would be nice, thank you. I can't close again today." He gave her a tight smile, and she knew his business may have suffered because of her.

She had to find a way to make it up to him. "Coffee?"

"Definitely." She watched his back as he disappeared down the hallway and unlocked the door to the store.

"Pa-pa." Rosie wanted out of the carriage, but wanted her father. Or was it Cecil she wanted? It was difficult to tell. What she did know was Rosie would never know her biological parents, and that was incredibly sad.

Hannah had not taken much from the Richardson house except for Rosie's clothes and other necessities, but she did take something that didn't belong to her. Until now she'd regretted it.

She'd tucked the ornate frame underneath the mattress in the baby carriage. It was the only photograph she had managed to find with both Rosie's parents. When she was old enough, she would be given the photograph, and learn about her parents.

Hannah didn't know a lot about them, she mainly knew them from church. But they were good people, and didn't deserve to die so young. Little Rosemary didn't deserve to be left an orphan either.

If she hadn't taken her as the police officer suggested, she'd be laying in a cold, dank orphanage right now. It was the last thing she wanted for her, or for any child.

She picked the baby up and hugged her tight. She earned a big sloppy kiss for her troubles. Hannah's heart filled with warmth.

After changing and feeding her, Hannah put Rosie down for a nap.

Next she would tackle Cecil's lunch. She had no idea what food was available to her, and checked the pantry. There wasn't a great deal there, but she could make him a plate of beans, or a ham and cheese sandwich. There was also a small amount of bacon.

That was pretty much the extent of the supplies. She would make do today, but needed to get more supplies. Surely he wouldn't mind if she raided his Mercantile to fill their pantry?

She checked on Rosie, who was sleeping soundly in the spare room, then quietly went into the Mercantile with Cecil's luncheon. A sandwich would have to suffice today – it would be awkward eating beans out in the store.

He was serving a customer when she opened the door. Several other customers were also in the store.

All eyes turned to her. He grinned, and she felt like shrinking into the floor. "Everyone," he said when she got closer. "This is Hannah, my wife." He put an arm around her shoulder, and warmth flooded her.

She was certain it was all for display. There were no feelings between them, and that's the way he obviously wanted it to stay.

She heard the collective gasp from around the room. "Hello everyone," she said quietly, trying to sound confident but sure she'd failed.

"Here is your food," she said, leaving it on the shelf behind the counter. "I'll bring your coffee in a moment." She leaned in and whispered. "Rosie is napping."

He nodded, and returned to his customers.

Hannah returned a short time later with his mug of coffee, and Cecil snatched it up, apparently in urgent need of its sustenance. She smiled – she never could understand the reasoning behind coffee desperation.

By the time she returned, the store was empty of customers. "We need supplies if I'm to make supper tonight."

"Of course," he said, grabbing a large box from under the counter. "I'll help. Anything you want, put in this box."

They wandered around the store and she added flour, sugar, eggs, and milk. "I'll make pancakes tonight. Do you have fruit and vegetable here?"

"I carry most things here, but not meat. The butcher is up the road, and you can put whatever you need on my account."

"I have a bit of money," she told him defiantly.

He looked annoyed. "You are my wife, and I will provide for you. Put your purchases on my account," he said firmly. She nodded and continued to fill the box with her immediate requirements. "Anything you need, you come out here and take it. No need to ask."

She nodded again, but didn't feel comfortable with this arrangement – it almost felt like stealing.

Should she tell him how she feels? Hannah decided not to since he was already annoyed with her.

He carried the box into the residence for her and placed it on the table. As he turned to leave, they heard Rosie giggling.

She headed to the bedroom and he followed. Luckily the store was devoid of customers. It got Hannah to wondering if he'd ever left the store unattended before.

"What about your customers?" She leaned into the carriage and pulled a very wet baby out. She had already laid a towel on the spare bed, and now lay the giggling child there.

"The bell over the door will alert me to any customers." He tickled Rosie under the chin. "What a good little girl you are," he said as he continued to tickle her.

"Pa-pa."

He glanced up at Hannah. "Is that the only word she can say?"

"She can say 'ted-ted' when she wants her toy teddy bear."

Right on queue, likely because she'd heard it said, the word flowed from her mouth. "Ted-ted." Her little arms outstretched, and Cecil glanced about trying to locate the toy in question.

"It's in the carpetbag," Hannah told him. "It's one of the few toys I managed to bring. I already had far too much baggage." It didn't make her happy, far from it, but a decision had to be made at the time.

He pulled the toy from the bag and handed it to a still giggling baby. "Ted-ted." Her little arms outstretched, she pulled the toy to herself and hugged it tightly.

A knot formed in Hannah's stomach. She would never regret having saved this sweet little girl from the awful fate of an orphanage. She was a happy baby, but that would have quickly changed if she'd been placed in such an institution.

"She's quite happy playing there, isn't she?"

Hannah knew it wasn't a question, but she answered anyway. "She's mostly happy, provided she's fed and dry."

Hannah lifted Rosie up and she reached out to Cecil. He had begun to hug her when the bell over the shop door tinkled. "I'm sorry, little one," he said, regret in his voice. "But Papa has to go to work."

He handed her over and scurried back to the store.

Papa? Did that mean he was already accepting Rosie as his daughter? With all her heart, Hannah certainly hoped so.

Chapter Five

Cecil closed the store for the day. He really wanted to stay and stack the shelves with the latest delivery items, but it had been a long day, and he was exhausted.

He pondered it was likely more emotional exhaustion than physical.

As he opened the door to the residence, the aroma of cooking food assaulted his senses. He hadn't eaten a real meal for a very long time. Except at the diner.

Mrs Baker prided herself on home-cooked meals, and he visited at least once a fortnight. The rest of the time he had canned beans, scrambled eggs, or sometimes, for a change he had bacon and eggs on toast.

He had no idea what supper involved, as Hannah had taken a large variety of foods to restock the pantry. He'd been rather negligent in that area for as long as he could remember. But what was the point when he didn't like to cook?

She stood at the wood stove her back to him, and the sight stirred something in him. Was it just through having a woman in the house?

He'd left her to her own devices today, not wanting to interfere with whatever she was doing. It was more so she could get used to her new home and get settled in without interruption more than anything. Rosie was the same – she especially needed to explore her new environment. It must be a difficult change, particularly for the baby.

He cleared his throat, not wanting to startle her. "Oh!" She turned with a spoon in her hand, and flour across one cheek.

He grinned, then reached out to wipe the flour away. A thrill went down his spine, and he tried to ignore it. "You have flour on your face," he said as he chuckled. "What are you making?"

She turned back to the stove. "Pancakes with potatoes and bacon. I'll make something more substantial tomorrow." She glanced over her shoulder at him. "I hope that's alright?"

"It's more than alright," he said into her ear, breathing in the fragrance he'd also noticed earlier. Lavender water if his senses told him correctly.

He leaned over her shoulder to glance at the food, but it only made it worse. Her nearness was something he should be avoiding. He stepped back and out of the danger zone. "Where's Rosie?" A change of subject was probably his best protection.

"I've already fed her, and now she's sleeping." Disappointment flood him. Did that mean he wouldn't get to see her again tonight? "Supper's ready."

He shook his disappointment aside and sat when instructed. Hannah put a plate of food in front of him, and Cecil leaned in and breathed deeply. Heaven. "It smells wonderful," he said honestly.

The moment Hannah sat down, he reached for her hand, ready to say a prayer of thanks. He'd been lacking in that area for a long time. It didn't seem prudent to be thankful about food he barely tolerated, but tonight was different.

"Dear Lord," he said as he held her hand. "Thank you for this wonderful food. Amen."

"Amen."

He lifted his knife and fork and began to eat. He took a mouthful of the pancakes. It melted in his mouth. The potatoes and bacon were every bit as good. He glanced across to see her watching him. "This is really good," he said, about to take another mouthful.

She laughed. "Anyone would think you hadn't eaten in days."

"I guess I haven't - not real food anyway. Not like this," he said. "This is delicious."

She stared at him in apparent disbelief. "What have you been eating?" Her brows were drawn in a frown. He preferred her when she was smiling.

He waved his fork through the air. "You know, beans, eggs, bacon. Stuff like that."

Cecil couldn't help but hear her sigh, and he watched a sadness come over her. "I'm sorry to hear that," she said quietly. "As of today, all that changes."

He nodded. What else could he do? Tell his new wife she couldn't cook for him? That certainly wasn't going to happen.

"I put Rosie in the spare room to sleep. I hope that was alright." She glanced across at him, a worried expression on her pretty face. "Since you want a marriage in name only, I'll sleep in there too."

That took him by surprise. He was certain his new wife would sleep with him, but he realized it would be impractical. He was, after all, a normal man with normal urges.

He had no idea why he'd even said that. He wanted children of his own, but the shock of having Hannah arrive with a ready-made family had thrown him off kilter.

It was going to be difficult enough for her to manage the shop as well as a child, let alone a tribe of children. Life had been so much simpler before. *Why had he arranged for a mail order bride?*

Without thinking about it, Cecil knew the answer – he was lonely, and had been for a very long time. And now he'd blown it.

~*~

Hannah was ready for bed. She stared across at Cecil – the man she barely knew, who was now her husband.

He'd taken her luggage into his bedroom when she'd arrived, and now he didn't want her in his bed.

"What do you…"

"I've been thinking…"

They both spoke at once.

"You first." They spoke in unison again.

Ladies first," he got out before they clashed with their words again.

"I was going to say all my luggage is in your bedroom." She averted her eyes, not wanting to think about the implications of being in Cecil's room. "I don't want to risk waking Rosie taking it in there."

"Then go in there and get what you need for tonight. We can move the rest of your luggage in the morning."

So that was that. He really didn't want her in his bed. His words cut through her heart.

Hannah had come here with the expectation of being a wife in every sense of the word. Everything changed because she'd bought Rosie with her, but she didn't blame him.

She also didn't blame Rosie. There was no way she could have left that dear sweet child to such a horrible future. Her heartrate quickened just thinking about where she could be right now.

The vision of rats and other vermin crawling over the baby as she slept entered Hannah's mind and she cried out.

Cecil suddenly stood. "Are you alright?" He stepped toward her, and she leaned into him. His arms gingerly came up around her. Was he afraid to touch her?

"I had thoughts of Rosie in the orphanage." She stopped talking in case she broke down. The last thing she wanted was for her new husband to think she was weak.

"Shhhh," he said into her ear. "She's here, and she's safe." He stroked her hair and it felt good. "I won't let anything happen to her."

Hannah swallowed back a sob. "What if they try to take her away?"

He didn't speak for close to a minute, and it worried her. "No one knows she is here. Don't worry yourself over nothing."

His words calmed her and she felt far better. She wished they were sleeping together though, he had a calming way about him that always left her feeling better.

"Thank you," she whispered. "I guess I'd better go to bed now. Rosie is an early riser." She pulled out of his arms, and she felt suddenly bereft. It was a feeling she'd never experienced before.

He nodded, and she headed toward Cecil's bedroom to retrieve her nightgown and essential toiletries, such as her hairbrush.

Cecil stood in the doorway watching her every movement. He berated himself again for his thoughtless words.

Right now, watching his wife, the last thing he wanted was for her to go into another room and another bed.

He glanced across at the double bed in what was meant to be their wedding bed. He'd even changed the sheets this morning before he opened the store.

And then he turned around and opened his big mouth in a panic.

So what if they had more children? That's what he wanted, right? He cared little if she couldn't work in the store because of their babies. That was part of the plan.

Joe Hartley seemed happy enough with his little family, and his business hadn't suffered.

His eyes strayed back to Hannah. She seemed to be struggling with the opening on her trunk. "Here, let me." He reached in to help, and their hands met.

Hers were so soft and gentle, and a shiver went down his spine. He glanced up to see her staring at him. Surely she didn't feel that too?

With every moment that passed, he regretted his words. But now he had to live with them. Perhaps even for a lifetime.

After the worst sleep he'd had for a long time, Cecil strolled into the store to open up.

Thoughts of Hannah had overtaken his waking moments, as well as his fleeting dreams.

He felt less enthusiastic about going to work today than he had for a very long time. This was his livelihood, and he needed to up his game.

What was holding him back? Yesterday was his wedding day, and the day he'd gained a family. He should be ecstatic, but he wasn't. It was totally his fault.

And there it was.

He'd already become enamored with the tiny person who had insinuated herself into his heart without his consent. Those big brown eyes and those teeny hands that caressed his cheeks like he was someone important to her had pulled him in.

Then she'd gone and called him Papa, and his heart melted.

He shook himself. He couldn't think like that. What he needed was distance. Distance between himself and the two females who had forced their way into his life, and if he was truthful, his heart.

Hannah was everything she'd told him in her letters. She was also far more. As a single woman who'd recently had a small child foisted on her without warning, she was behaving more like the child's mother.

She was strong and capable, but she was also gentle and caring, and vulnerable. He was already enjoying her company.

It made him feel good inside.

But then he'd gone and messed it all up. He'd pushed her away, and if he was truthful with himself, pushed away the best thing that had come into his life in a very long time.

Hannah, his beautiful wife.

He glanced up as the bell over the door tinkled.

"Ah, Mrs Baker. Good morning to you."

She stared at him for long moments. "I'll just wander around if you don't mind," she told him, but Cecil knew her far too well.

The rumors had already started and she'd come here to confirm the story. She was a good woman, and would do anything for anybody, but she liked to have her finger on the pulse. If she didn't know what was going on, it wasn't worth knowing.

"I'll take these six kitchen towels," she said when she arrived back at the front counter. "I also need some dish cloths, but I couldn't find any on the shelf."

"I know I have some," Cecil said, on the alert for the subject of his marriage to come up. "Oh, I remember now," he said after a bit of thought. "They arrived yesterday. Let me get them from the storeroom."

He came back soon afterwards with a box of dish cloths and placed some on the counter. "Are these for the Diner? How many did you want?"

She looked down at them. "Yes, for the Diner. I'll take six for now. Perhaps I might take another six kitchen towels too."

He began to walk through the store to collect the additional items and could sense Mrs Baker behind him.

"I heard you married yesterday, Mr Delbert. Congratulations." It must have killed her to wait so long to ask. He knew she would eventually, but it had to be the right time.

He smiled, then turned to face her. "Why, yes, I did Mrs Baker." He grabbed six more of the requested items, then they headed back to the counter together.

"Hannah is my wife. She had a very long trip to get here." He knew she was dying to ask how they met, but also knew she wouldn't. She would find out eventually, somehow.

Mrs Baker didn't have a mean bone in her body, so her questions didn't irritate him, but they did amuse him.

He opened the account book and wrote her purchases against her business account. His head turned as the door to the residence opened.

"Papa!" The little voice carried throughout the store, and he cringed inwardly. He had no idea why, except he didn't feel like explaining himself right now.

"Ooooh, what a dear child," Mrs Baker said, rushing over to the newcomers. "You didn't tell me you have a baby, Mr Delbert," she said accusingly.

"I, I'm sorry," Hannah said quickly. "I'm interrupting. I just need some potatoes for supper."

Mrs Baker outstretched her arms to hold Rosie. "Do you mind?" she asked Hannah. "I have no children of my own, and I adore babies."

"Of course not," Hannah replied.

Rosie went straight to her and hugged the older woman tightly. "She is very sweet," Mrs Baker said. "What is the dear child's name?"

"Rosemary, but everyone calls her Rosie."

"Such a beautiful name. I'm Edna Baker, by the way."

She glanced across at Cecil and he knew he was being reprimanded for not introducing them. "This is my wife Hannah," he finally said. "I'll just get the potatoes for you." He slunk away and leaving the two women to talk.

"I always knew you had a kind heart, Mr Delbert," she said when he returned, obviously fully aware of the plight of little Rosie. "You'll make an excellent father."

She handed the baby back to Hannah, then took her purchases and turned away.

"Thank you, Mrs Baker," he said, meaning for her purchase, but perhaps she took it to mean for her kind words.

Was that tears he saw in the woman's eyes? Surely not. She was a tough old bird.

The moment the door shut behind her, he turned to Hannah. "That's fixed the rumor mill. Everyone will want to meet you and Rosie now." He smiled, then chuckled. "I guess that's one way to spread the word."

"I'm sorry," Hannah said again. "I feel bad now, but I needed the extra supplies."

He took the baby who was reaching out to him. She planted a sloppy kiss on his cheek, and his heart raced. How could such a tiny creature cause all these feelings? Especially when he'd only met her yesterday.

He pulled her closer and hugged her. Warmth filled his very being. "Don't be sorry," he said, handing Rosie back. "I have to get back to work now. I had a delivery yesterday and haven't unpacked it yet."

Hannah looked down to the floor. "I was supposed to help you with things like that. I've messed everything up." Tears filled her eyes. Was the shock of what happened finally hitting her? He guided her into a chair behind the counter.

"You saved this beautiful girl's life. Instead of sending her to strangers, you took her on yourself."

She glanced up at him. "You don't mind?"

"I did at first," he admitted. "It was quite a shock to see you there with a baby carriage. But it's different now. We're a family."

He pulled her to her feet, and hugged her while she still held the baby. She was warm, gentle and strong all at the same time. He wanted to hold her forever.

Until he realized what he was doing.

He'd vowed not to make this a real marriage, but one of convenience. He would have help in the house, even if not in the store, and she would have the support of a husband.

It was a win/win situation. Or was it?

Rosie was finally asleep. She had a stew on for supper, she'd washed the diapers, and the house was clean.

Hannah decided to help Cecil in the store – at least until the baby woke up. She left the door slightly ajar so she'd hear if she cried.

Cecil smiled as she entered the Mercantile. "What are you doing out here?" he asked. He wasn't annoyed, going by his tone, just curious.

"Rosie is asleep, so I thought I'd help you."

His face lit up, and he handed her an apron. "I have a ton of stock that needs to go on the shelves." He guided her to the storeroom, then showed her where everything needed to go out in the store. "I'm not normally so far behind," he said. "But yesterday was rather out of the ordinary."

It was, for both of them. "Well, I can stay here until Rosie wakes up, then I have to go."

"That's all I ask. Let me know if you need anything."

He watched as she moved about the store familiarizing herself with the layout and stacking the shelves. Hannah could feel his gaze burning into her back. When she glanced over her shoulder to check, he suddenly turned his head. To hide his actions?

Most likely.

She had no idea why he'd made the decision to have a marriage of convenience. She should have pulled out when he'd told her that outside the church. But where was she to go?

Everything she did affected not only herself now, but Rosie too. And not going through with the marriage could have meant Rosie ended up...

No, she wouldn't even think about it.

She knew what it was like to be homeless. Life had been difficult for her – between her babysitting and Governess jobs, Hannah had been almost penniless. If it hadn't been for some very special friends, she would have been living on the streets.

It was the reason she'd decided to become a mail order bride. At twenty-six, she needed more stability in her life. A husband would do that.

Cecil seemed to like her. At least she wasn't abhorrent to him. When he'd held her, he seemed to genuinely care. Then suddenly his demeanor would change, and he would keep his distance. And now? He didn't seem to have any problem with her. It was the strangest thing.

The bell over the door tinkled, interrupting her thoughts.

"Good afternoon, Mrs Thompson." Cecil smiled at this customer, and she smiled back. "Can I help you with anything?"

She waved his offer aside. "I am in need of flour and some other bits and pieces. I'm happy to wander."

Hannah stood watching the exchange, but Cecil didn't introduce her. Again. Was he embarrassed by her? She hadn't thought so, but perhaps he just didn't like to talk to his customers about personal things.

"Oh, Mrs Thompson," he said finally. "This is my wife, Hannah."

The woman stepped back and gave him a look. One that said *when did that happen?*

"We were married yesterday," Cecil added, and Mrs Thompson nodded, as though that explained everything. Hannah walked to his side, and Cecil put his arm around her. It felt good, but she knew it was all for show – for the customer standing in the store right now.

She pulled off her apron the moment she heard the baby crying. That resulted in another look from Mrs Thompson. "You have a baby?"

Hannah shouldn't have been surprised. Cecil said word would have got around they'd married, but unless Mrs Baker managed to get the rest of the message across, people would talk. They always did.

She stared back at the two, torn between the awkward conversation and the welfare of her charge. Rosie's needs won. She glanced at her husband, who nodded gently. She had his blessing. Not that should would have stayed even if she didn't – the baby came first.

The crying suddenly stopped and Hannah guessed she was playing with her teddy. She ducked her head around the door to discover she was right.

Little eyes spotted her and the baby giggled, then her arms stretched out to be picked up. She laid her gently on the towel put there for that reason, and changed the wet diaper.

Rosie would be wanting a bottle – a rarity these days, but she liked one when she woke up from her afternoon nap. It wouldn't be long and everything would change.

At nearly six months old, there was so much she was on the cusp of doing. Then she would be a huge handful.

Hannah carried her out to the kitchen and prepared her bottle. Thankfully Cecil carried condensed milk, otherwise she didn't know what she would have done.

"Pa-pa," she called, wanting to see Cecil. She called repeatedly for him, so they went back out to the shop. Hannah ducked her head around the corner of the store to ensure there were no customers. "Pa-pa!" she shouted when she spotted him.

His face lit up, and he strolled toward them. "Sweet Rosie," he said, obviously happy to see her. She'd stopped drinking when she'd spotted him, but now shoved the bottle back in her mouth again.

Rosie had such a cute personality.

He leaned in and kissed the baby on the forehead.

Hannah could get very used to this. Get used to being a mother and a wife. If only things between her and Cecil were better, more intimate.

Chapter Seven

Rosie had been asleep for some hours, and Hannah enjoyed the time alone with Cecil.

They'd taken to stacking new stock on the shelves after hours. It wasn't ideal, but it was preferable to not helping at all. That was why she'd been brought here, after all.

Standing in the storeroom, Hannah looked up in despair. She couldn't reach the boxes of undergarments she needed, and was pondering what to do when Cecil entered the room. "Everything alright?" he asked.

She pointed upwards. "I can't reach." She wasn't short. Not compared to most women anyway. But neither was she tall.

Now Cecil, he was what you called tall. The top of her head only just reached his shoulder. She knew that because she'd rested it there on a few occasions. Not that he'd complained, but when they stood like that, she felt closer to her husband.

It had been nearly a week now since they'd arrived, but he wouldn't let himself get closer. Sure, he liked to play with Rosie, and made a point of doing so several times a day. But the moment the two of them seemed to be anything that could be described as intimate – even a hug – he pulled away before it could develop into anything else.

It was disheartening.

He reached up and handed her the boxes. Placing them in her hands, she felt the warmth of his skin. Her hands lingered longer than they should. He stared at her for long moments.

Did he feel the connection she felt? When he was near she felt good, and warmth flooded her body. When he touched her, a shiver went down her spine.

Any sort of physical connection caused her nerve endings to be on high alert.

Hannah wasn't sure what it all meant, but she knew one thing – she felt dejected, and hankered for more affection from her husband.

She shoved past him and headed out into the store to do the job he wanted his wife to do. She restocked the shelves.

After that she strolled through the store checking if any other stocks were low. She stopped when she got to the toiletries section. The soap needed refilling, and so did the hair brushes. She'd seen them in the storeroom, so headed back there.

Cecil was in there checking the stock levels. She had to reach past him to get to the soaps. As she did so, she brushed against his bare arm.

A shiver went through her entire body, and she turned to face him. "Sorry," she said under her breath.

He moved toward the back of the storeroom, forcing her to move there too. "I'm not," he said gently, then leaned in and brushed his lips against hers.

Before she knew what was happening, he had deepened the kiss, then suddenly pulled back as though her skin had burned him.

Hannah looked up at him, then touched her fingers to her tingling lips.

"I, I shouldn't have done that," he said, and stormed out, leaving her to stare after him.

He was already gone by the time she found her voice. "Don't be sorry," she whispered. But it was too late.

It had been a week since that kiss. The one he'd longed for from the moment Hannah had arrived.

But he'd been so embarrassed about his lack of restraint, he'd stormed out, not daring to wait for her response.

Cecil knew from the moment the words were out at their wedding, he'd pushed himself into a corner. It had been his decision to make theirs a marriage of convenience, not Hannah's and now he regretted it.

She hadn't protested at his declaration, so now he had no choice but to live with his decision. Having her there in the same house made it impossible to avoid her, which made the task far more challenging.

Every time he walked into the kitchen he noticed her curves. When she smiled, which was most of the time, he zoned in on her lips. And when she brushed by him, his body reacted.

Cecil did not want to continue like this, but didn't want to admit he'd been wrong.

He enjoyed her company, and tried to spend as much time as possible with her, despite the hardship it caused him.

Hardship because he couldn't hold her in his arms and kiss her again.

He glanced down at Rosie who was playing at his feet. Supper was over, and it was almost time for bed for the little one. He hated missing her at the end of the day, so the routine had been changed so he could spend time with her before bed.

"Pa-pa." Her little arms went up for him to pick her up. He leaned in to do so when suddenly she changed position. She rolled over and sat up!

She was a little wobbly, and almost toppled backwards, but she sat up.

"Hannah, look," he said, indicating the child on the floor.

She glanced up and grinned. "How wonderful," she said, quite animated. "It won't be long and she will be crawling."

"Crawling?" That was a whole different scenario. When that happened she'd be in to everything. "I've been thinking," he said. "Rosie can't sleep in that carriage forever. She'll grow out of it soon anyway. Tomorrow we'll check the catalogs and order a crib for her."

"That's a good idea. I have money to pay for it." She stared at him, goading him to protest. "I have money from Mr Richardson."

Cecil gritted his teeth. "I can provide for our daughter," he said, his mood suddenly darker.

She straightened her shoulders. "I know that," she said gently. "But what am I to do with this money?"

As much as he felt aggrieved, what she said made perfect sense, but still he wanted to be the one to look after them. "How much are we talking about?"

Her voice was barely above a whisper. "About thirty dollars." She fidgeted with her hands. "It was as though he knew something might happen to him."

Cecil thought for a moment. "Alright. I'll allow it this time, only because I can see you're distressed."

She stood, and sighed as she did, obviously relieved. "If there's enough, perhaps we could order a stroller and high chair too?"

That was a good idea. With the baby sitting up, it could come in handy. He lifted Rosie from the floor. "Time for bed now baby." He pulled her in for a hug, then held her away from himself. "Someone needs a change of diaper."

Hannah laughed then took the baby. "We'll come back for you to say goodnight," she said, her hands brushing his. He wanted to reach out and pull her to him, but with a wet baby between them, it wasn't such a good idea.

When he thought about it, perhaps it wasn't a good idea at all. The last thing he wanted was to break his self-imposed pact. Once broken, there'd be no turning back. He knew how he felt about Hannah, but had no idea of her feelings toward him.

She hadn't been gone long when she returned with a dry baby. Hannah handed her over, and a shiver went down his body. Their skin to skin connection was driving him crazy. Whenever they touched he yearned for her even more.

He looked down into Rosie's eyes. She stared up at him then grinned. She wriggled about until he lifted her for a hug. "Goodnight, Rosie," he said gently.

Now he'd had them in his life, Cecil couldn't imagine how he survived without his family. But he wanted to be a real family. He didn't like the way they danced around each other – it was breaking his heart.

"I'll put her down," he said. "When I come back we need to talk."

Hannah chewed on her bottom lip with worry. "Nothing is wrong," he said, then left the room.

When he returned Hannah was perched on the edge of the sitting room chair, her hands twisting in her lap.

"I told you not to worry," he said, agitated with himself for causing her concern. "I had an idea, and want your opinion." She looked relieved.

She followed him out to the store. "This corner is rather useless," he said, pulling some old boxes from the area. "It's used for rubbish and not much more."

Hannah stared at him, her expression one of confusion. "I thought we could make it a play area for Rosie," he said. "If we clean it out, I could get some dowel and she would be contained."

Her eyes opened wide. "That's a brilliant idea," she said, apparently now on the same page. "We could put some toys in there, and now that she's sitting up, it would keep her happy."

"Exactly. She wouldn't get under our feet, so she'd be safe, and we can see what she's doing." He took both her hands. The moment they touched he knew he shouldn't have done it.

"Cecil," she said softly.

He stepped back. "I'm sorry," he said. "I didn't mean to overstep."

She looked disappointed. "Overstep? You're my husband." She turned away from him. "But you don't act that way. Am I so ugly that you can't stand to touch me?"

He heard her voice crack and it broke his heart. He moved toward her and wrapped his arms around her from behind. "You're not ugly," he said gently. "You are the most beautiful woman I know."

His heart hammered at their closeness, and he wanted to be closer still.

"Then why do you keep your distance from me?" Hot tears dripped onto his hands which were still around her. "Why do you force me to sleep alone?"

Before he had a chance to answer, she broke away and ran back into the residence. He could hear her sobbing from the store.

This wasn't what he wanted, far from it. He was trying to protect her. He was a man who worked long hours, he was rarely home. As it was, he barely got to see Hannah and little Rosie, and it broke his heart.

Besides, most women didn't take to him, didn't like his old fashioned ways. He'd been out with a few women during his life, but it always ended after just a few dates and they ended up marrying someone else.

He had worked in the store most of his life, and inheriting it from his father had seemed a blessing at the time, but now he saw it as more of a burden.

He wanted a wife in every sense of the word, and he wanted a family. Well, he had a family already but he wasn't playing fair. Deep in his heart he knew this was all of his doing.

Hannah was still sobbing, and he didn't know what to do. Should he go to her and try to console her, or leave her to believe him the monster that he truly was?

This was all his fault – he was the one who requested a mail order bride. And he was the one who hadn't abided by the rules. Pushing her away was not part of the deal.

He had to find a way to make it right.

Hannah brushed the tears from her eyes. She must look as ugly as what Cecil seemed to think she already was.

Right now it felt like the biggest mistake of her life was coming here. But Rosie needed a stable home, and marrying Cecil Delbert had seemed the right choice.

She shook her head. She shouldn't be thinking like this – he was a good man, that was more than obvious.

He'd taken to Rosie almost from the moment she'd forced him to hold her. The child had a contagious personality. Once you had exposure to her, you simply couldn't get enough.

Unfortunately, the same couldn't be said for herself.

She lay on the bed in the spare room and pondered her future. Hannah couldn't envisage herself enduring this situation for the rest of her life. She had to make a decision about her future. Their future – hers and Rosie's.

It wouldn't be easy, she knew that, but neither was the position she found herself in now. She fully understood when deciding to be a mail order bride it wouldn't be easy. But she didn't for a moment believe it would be this difficult.

In his letters, Cecil had come across as a loving man, and one who would be affectionate toward her. She'd certainly seen glimpses of that, but they were short lived.

She couldn't think of a single thing she'd done to cause that situation. When she thought about it some more she had to wonder. Why was a fully-grown man of thirty-two years old still unmarried?

Surely he'd courted some of the women in town?

Or perhaps he hadn't. He worked long hours. Far longer than he needed to work, she was more than certain.

And the whole purpose of their marriage, in his view anyway, was for her to help him out and shorten his work day.

So far that hadn't happened, all because she'd bought a child with her.

The thought made her eyes well up again. Rosie was not a burden. At least not to her. Hannah couldn't have lived with herself if she'd allowed the baby to be placed in an orphanage.

The thought made her cry out and she began to sob again.

Without warning she was wrapped in warm arms. Cecil was lying on the bed next to her, holding her tight. "I'm sorry," he said gently. "I'm the worst husband in the entire world."

His voice broke, and she knew he was as unhappy about their situation as she was. "Please don't cry," he said, handing her a clean handkerchief.

She felt him shift on the bed to move closer still. "I'm sorry things haven't worked out as well as we'd hoped," he said, and her heart shattered.

Hannah knew what was coming. He was breaking up with her. He would arrange for an annulment and would send her away.

She braced for his next words.

"Everything happened back-to-front. We had a child before we got to know each other," And here it comes, she thought, her heart thudding in her chest.

"Starting now, I am going to court you." He pulled her even tighter against himself. "I really like you, Hannah," he said quietly. "I knew it before we even met. Your letters told me everything I needed to know."

She was speechless. This was far from what she expected. "I, I like you too," she squeaked, her voice not cooperating.

He leaned over and looked into her face. "You don't sound too sure."

Tears rolled down her already blotchy face. "I thought you were going to send us away." She began to sob again, she couldn't help it. Relief flooded her body and the sobs just pushed their way out.

He rolled her to face him, and she covered her face with her hands. "Don't look at me, I'm ugly from crying," she said.

"You could never be ugly," he said, his voice breaking. "You're the most beautiful woman I know."

Hannah pulled her hands away and stared at him. "I thought you hated me," she said softly. "I was certain I must be repulsive to you."

He pulled her up and wrapped his arms around her. "That could never happen," he said. "I am in love with you."

Surely he didn't mean that? If he was in love with her why did he constantly push her way? "Then why…?"

"Because I was scared of getting too close." His head came down and he brushed his lips gently across hers. When she didn't object, Cecil deepened the kiss.

Perhaps they could make this work after all.

#

Hannah got herself and Rosie ready for church. It was a beautiful day, and it was such a pity it would be wasted.

Cecil was not one for socializing, or for even going out for a stroll. Hannah loved them. She loved being around people, but since she'd arrived, she'd barely done either.

She knew Rosie loved going out too, and now she could sit up, even though she was still a little wobbly without support, she would be sure to like it even more.

They chose and ordered the crib and a stroller. They also ordered a high chair in preparation for what would soon be their future; Rosie sitting up unassisted. She longed for their arrival. It would be so much better for Rosie. She was an inquisitive baby, and having a stroller would be perfect for her. The high chair would make meal times easier too.

She pulled on her bonnet, and picked Rosie up. "You look so pretty," she said, hugging the baby to her. As she pulled back, Rosie pulled on the ribbons of her bonnet. "Don't do that, Rosie," she said gently. She was after all a baby and didn't know better.

"Are you getting up to mischief," Cecil asked his daughter, then took her from his wife. "Mama doesn't like that," he said as he chuckled.

"Mama?" It wasn't something she'd heard him say before, but yes, she guessed she was Mama now.

He frowned. "Of course. If I can be Papa, then you can definitely be Mama." He pulled out his pocket-watch. "If you're ready, we'd best leave. We don't want to be late for church."

He placed Rosie in the carriage, a pillow at her back so she could see everything, and they were soon on their way.

Once outside, Hannah put her face toward the sun. "It is beautiful out here," she said. "I love the feel of the sun on my face, and the fresh air makes me feel alive."

He looked at her thoughtfully. "It's good for you, and the baby. You should go out more."

She nodded and as much as she'd love to do that, she'd much prefer to go with her husband coming along with them. But apparently he didn't like the outdoors much.

As they strolled along the wooden boardwalk of the main street, she looked about. She hadn't seen much of Grand Falls. Most of the time she'd either been helping in the store, cooking, or looking after Rosie.

Not that she was complaining. Her life was far better since she'd arrived here. She had stability, she knew where she was sleeping on a daily basis, and she had a husband. Now all she needed was for Cecil to see her as his wife, and not just someone who had come to help him out.

As much as he'd promised to change that, she was still on edge. She swallowed back the emotion that threatened to overtake her. Hannah fought hard – she would not arrive at church all red-eyed and face blotchy.

The last of the parishioners were making their way inside as they arrived. Mrs Baker was there and turned back when she heard the giggling sounds of Rosie.

"Sweet Rosemary," she said, calling the baby by her full name. Rosie's arms stretched out to be picked up.

"Not now, Rosie," Cecil told her. "Perhaps later." She went back to playing with her teddy.

The organ music began and they all shuffled through the door. Cecil chose a pew near the back so Hannah could make a quick exit if the baby became restless.

Mrs Baker sat beside them and quietly played with the baby as the music continued. It was obvious to Hannah the woman adored babies.

Preacher Devon entered the church and welcomed everyone, then bowed his head in prayer. The congregation did the same. As they recited The Lord's Prayer, Rosie could be heard loudly calling her

Papa. A few chuckles could be heard around the room.

When they were finished, everyone sat down. Pastor Devon spoke. "It is refreshing to have a talkative young child with us today. He looked about until he spotted her, then strolled over to where they sat.

The pastor lightly touched Rosie's head. "Bless you, Rosemary," he said, then walked up the front of the church again to resume the service.

It warmed Hannah's heart that the preacher would do such a thing. This sweet soul needed all the blessings she could get.

Standing out the front of the church with the rest of the parishioners, Mrs Baker came over to the little family. "That was so nice of Pastor Devon," she said. "Although I wouldn't expect anything less. He's a wonderful man."

"Yes, he is," Cecil said. "Shall we go inside for coffee?"

Hannah jumped at the chance. She didn't know many of the town's people, and this was a way for her to meet them. He cupped her elbow and led her into the hall, lifting the carriage up the steps.

"Rosemary needs a stroller," Mrs Baker said gently. "She is nearly old enough to sit up."

Hannah grinned. "She is beginning to sit up already, when she wants to, and we have a stroller ordered."

"How wonderful." The older woman clapped her hands and grinned. "You must bring her to visit me at the diner sometime soon. We could have coffee and a chat."

How lovely would that be? It was the first invitation Hannah had received since arriving. "I'd really like that, Mrs Baker. Thank you," she said.

Cecil came over with a cup of tea for Hannah and an oatmeal cookie for Rosie. The latter was snatched out of his hand when he got it close to her little hands.

They all laughed. "She's probably getting hungry," Hannah said. "I usually give her stewed fruit for luncheon, then she has a bottle and a nap."

"She seems such a good baby," Mrs Baker said. "You are very lucky after everything she's been through."

"My daughter is an exemplary baby," he said.

The two women looked at each other and laughed. "Of course she is," Mrs Baker said, still trying to control her mirth.

"So, what's on the agenda this afternoon," she asked. "A stroll around town, a ride through the countryside? I'm sure both your ladies would enjoy an afternoon with you."

"We usually stock shelves while Rosie is sleeping," Hannah offered.

Mrs Baker looked horrified. "Sunday is the only day your store is closed, Mr Delbert. Why on earth aren't you spending it doing something special with your family?"

Cecil's eyebrows joined. "That's a very good question, Mrs Baker," he said, then looked thoughtful. "Perhaps we could do something special this afternoon."

"That would be lovely," Hannah said, excited about the prospect of being outside for the afternoon. "What do you have in mind?"

"If I can arrange a buggy, we shall take a ride through the hillside."

That sounded wonderful, and she told her husband so. She was excited to spend time with him and get to know him better.

She took a sip of her tea, then glanced down at Rosie who was making a huge mess with the oatmeal cookie. They were both having a wonderful time.

Cecil clapped his hands as he entered the kitchen.

"I managed to arrange a buggy for the afternoon. We can have a picnic if we take sandwiches..." He stopped talking when he glanced across at Hannah. "Oh."

He should have known she would be well prepared – she was almost finished packing their picnic lunch.

82

"I figured we could still eat it if we couldn't go on a picnic." She thought of everything. "I made blueberry muffins last night, so I've packed some of those too."

He took the few steps to reach her, then kissed her forehead. "You are so organized and think of everything."

Last night had been difficult. She was so upset at his lack of affection, and Cecil was not going to allow that to happen again. It had broken his heart in two to see Hannah so incredibly distraught.

"I have already given Rosie some stewed apple, and warmed her bottle. She can have it when we get there."

He nodded his approval. Today would be the beginning of their new life together, and he would ensure his little family was happy. "The buggy is out back, so when you're ready, we can leave."

"Papa!" Rosie was animated as usual, and hearing her call his name warmed his heart. He could imagine what it would do to Hannah to be called Mama.

"Say *Mama*," he prompted. "*Mama*." Rosie stared at him, but persistence was the key, he was certain. "*Mama*. Say *Mama*."

She foisted a fist in her mouth.

"*Mama*." He would say it repeatedly until she got the gist of it. "*Mama*."

"Leave the poor child alone," Hannah told him. She seemed a tad annoyed.

"*Mama*," he said again, ignoring her plea. "*Mama*."

"Ma," Rosie said. "Ma-ma."

Hannah's eyes opened wide, and tears brimmed in her eyes. "See, I told you she'd get it," he said, more than a little elated at the outcome.

He lifted Rosie out of the carriage, then pushed her away from himself. "She's on the nose," he said gruffly. "Once you fix that, we'll go."

Hannah scowled but took the baby and left the room. He really needed to learn how to change diapers, but if he was honest with himself, it wasn't something he was interested in learning.

"All done," Hannah said as they returned. She snatched the baby bottle off the table and placed it in the picnic basket. "We're ready now."

"Give Papa a hug," he told Rosie, and she leaned over to comply. "Now give Mama a hug," he said, and Rosie hugged him again.

Hannah shrugged her shoulders as though it didn't matter, but he knew she was hurting. Rosie could say the word but had no idea what it meant. It would take time, but he vowed to remedy the situation.

Cecil carried the picnic basket out to the buggy while Hannah carried the baby. He put the basket up the back, then she climbed up while he held Rosie. Disappointment swept through him.

Cecil would have loved to lift her up, to hold her by the waist, and have her lips close to his – so close he could feel her breath.

But it wasn't to be. There would be other ways for them to be close, and he would take advantage of them as they presented themselves to him.

The Good Lord had put them together, and now it was up to Cecil to make it work. All blame lay with him for what had occurred, and he must fix it.

His wife was unhappy, and that made him unhappy. He was certain that feeling would be passed onto Rosie too.

He climbed up on the buggy and shuffled across until his knees were resting next to Hannah's. It felt good.

"Ya!" He flicked the reins and the horse moved forward. It's hooves clattered down the cobblestone back street and out of the town. Cecil guided it toward the hills. "We won't go far today," he said, glancing across at her. "There's a clearing near the river. It's a nice spot for a picnic."

He knew it to be a place where young men took the women they were courting, even though they shouldn't. It was a quiet spot, very isolated, but as a married couple he had no compunction about going there.

By the time they arrived about twenty minutes later, Rosie was becoming restless.

"She wants her bottle and a nap," Hannah told him.

He pulled up near some trees and wrapped the reins around a branch. He reached for a blanket he'd brought along for them to sit on and flicked it across the ground. Then he took Rosie and lay her down.

This was the moment he was looking forward to – holding Hannah by her waist and lifting her down to the ground. As he turned around, she was endeavoring to climb down herself.

"Hannah," he said. His voice sounding raspy, even to him. "Let me."

She turned back to face him, her expression confused. "I'm your husband. I want to help you down," he said.

He held his hands to her waist and his heart skipped a beat. As he lifted her off the wagon, time stood still. He gently lifted her toward the ground until they were face-to-face.

He breathed in – the fragrance of her lavender water filled his senses. The pull of her soft lips was more than he could bear. "Hannah," he said softly, then moved his face closer.

Their lips met and his head exploded. All he wanted right now was his wife. Kissing her was absolute bliss. She tasted of warm tea, and he wanted, needed more.

"Mama."

Rosie's voice interrupted him. He couldn't think of a more inopportune time for her to say the words he'd been coaching her to say.

"Mama."

She was sitting up watching them, and it made him chuckle. They would soon have no privacy, not that it mattered now, but he had high hopes for the future.

He gently put Hannah to the ground, then reached for the picnic basket. "She probably wants her bottle," Hannah said. "It's still warm," she said, handing it to the baby who was able to feed herself these days.

They sat together on the blanket and ate. "It's lovely here, Cecil. Thank you for bringing me."

He reached across and covered her hand, and much to his surprise, she didn't pull it away. "It is lovely. We must come again." He breathed in the fresh air.

"Do you hear that," she asked.

He listened but could hear nothing but the water as it rippled along the stream. "I hear nothing," he said, listening more intently.

She jumped up off the blanket. "Exactly. Shall we sit by the stream? Rosie is asleep," she said. "We can keep an eye on her from there."

He nodded. That would be nice. How long had it been since he'd been this far from the Mercantile? Six months? A year? It had to be at least two years –

perhaps even longer. He could not allow that to happen again.

His entire life had revolved around the Mercantile since his father had died. No, that was wrong, it was longer than that. Probably since he'd come of age.

He should have known better. Father had literally killed himself because he never once took a break. Cecil was heading the same way.

But now he had a purpose, now he had a family to look after. "Thank you for coming here today," he said as they headed toward the edge of the water. "We must come again some time soon."

"Yes, we must." She turned her head to glance at him, and their faces almost touched. Cecil wrapped his arms around her and pulled her close. Suddenly, his lips covered hers.

"I've been a fool," he whispered when they pulled apart for air.

Hannah rested her head on his shoulder. "Yes, you have, but I'm glad you finally came to your senses."

They stood there for what seemed forever. He glanced back to see Rosie was still sound asleep. Cecil couldn't believe that just weeks ago he was a confirmed bachelor, with no thought of children. Here he was now with a wife he cared deeply for, and a young daughter.

What the future held for them he didn't know, but provided his family were with him, he really didn't mind.

Chapter Nine

Locking the door to the store, Cecil removed his apron and hung it up. "Did I tell you I've made a booking at the diner," he asked as Hannah entered the store.

She looked annoyed. "No you didn't. Luckily I haven't already prepared something for supper."

"I'm sorry, I'll be certain to tell you next time. That was inconsiderate of me."

She stared at him. Did that sound insincere? He didn't mean it to seem that way.

He'd told Hannah he was going to court her, and that's exactly what he intended to do. Instead of spending their evening restocking the Mercantile, he would take his wife and child to the diner.

Neither of them should be spending their every waking moments working. He'd seen what it had done to his father, and he didn't want to see his wife go down that road, not to mention himself.

It wouldn't help their daughter one little bit to have no parents as she was growing up. It was bad enough her natural parents had died. She already had that to deal with as the years rolled on. He wouldn't burden her further.

Suddenly Hannah smiled and his world seemed brighter. "I'll go and freshen up," she said, then turned tail and headed back into the residence.

He stared after her. He'd been so lucky he was the one she'd chosen. It made him wonder where he'd be right now if he hadn't been her choice.

One thing was certain, he wouldn't have a bubbly little daughter. Cecil had never pictured himself as a father, but now he couldn't picture himself without his two wonderful girls.

He finished closing up and headed into the residence. Hannah's lavender water fragrance lingered and he breathed it in. She was the fresh air in his life, and he wondered how he'd survived all these years without her.

She came out of the bathroom carrying Rosie, who had a grin on her face. "Papa," she said, reaching out her arms. He grabbed her as she near jumped out of her mother's arms, then hugged him tight. She gave him a sloppy kiss on the cheek.

He put her in the baby carriage, then looked his wife up and down. "You look beautiful," he said holding her by the waist, then leaned in and kissed her on the cheek, secretly wishing for more.

Pushing the carriage, they left the residence and headed for the diner.

Mrs Baker welcomed them warmly, as Cecil knew she would. "Hello sweet Rosemary," she said, tickling the baby under the chin. She was rewarded with a series of giggles.

She showed them to a table where the carriage wouldn't be in the way, and handed them both menus. "Hearty Beef Stew with hot bread rolls is always a favorite," she told them. "Steak and vegetables is tonight's special."

They placed their orders, Hannah ordered the stew, and Cecil the steak. As she was about to turn away, she paused. "I'll bring some mashed vegetables for Rosemary, if that's alright?"

"Thank you," Hannah said graciously. "That would be wonderful."

She quickly returned with the food for Rosie, and placed a high chair at their table. Cecil placed the child in the chair, and Hannah began to feed her. The baby looked about. Everything must look so different to her from that height.

She seemed amazed, and somewhat distracted, but ate her food without issue. Cecil was so pleased they'd ordered a high chair, and could see what a difference it would make.

Once the baby had finished eating, Hannah cleaned the high chair as best she could and placed some toys in front of Rosie. Not long afterwards, their food arrived.

"It looks and smells wonderful, Mrs Baker," Hannah said, leaning in.

She was right, the aroma was more than a little enticing.

"Enjoy," Mrs Baker said, and then was gone.

"Are you enjoying yourself," Cecil asked, concerned she may not be, since she needed to look after Rosie as well.

She glanced up at him. "I certainly am," she said. "The food is delicious too."

They ate the rest of their meal in silence. When they finished, Cecil slid his hand across the table and covered hers. "I've really enjoyed our night together," he said. "We'll have to do it more often."

"But the cost…" she whispered.

He didn't care about the cost. It wasn't that expensive anyway. Besides, until Hannah and the baby arrived, he had nothing to spend his money on. This was far more enjoyable than stockpiling his profits in the local bank.

He shook his head. "Nothing to worry about," he said.

Soon after, Mrs Baker arrived and packed up their dishes. "For dessert tonight we have peach cobbler or apple pie – both with clotted cream."

"I'll have peach cobbler, thank you Mrs Baker," Cecil answered. "What about you, Hannah?"

She patted her belly. "I don't think I could eat another thing."

"Two peach cobblers it is then, Mrs Baker," he said. When she protested, he added, "If you really don't want it, I'm sure Rosie will eat some of it." He grinned and Mrs Baker's eyes lit up. She was always commenting how the younger women of today were far too thin.

When the desserts arrived, Hannah began to feed hers to Rosie, who loved it. When she'd had enough, Hannah took a mouthful. "Oooh, this is really good," she said, and ate the remainder of the food in the bowl.

He didn't say anything as he didn't want to embarrass her, but was very pleased he'd ordered it despite her protests.

They soon stood and both stretched after having sat for so long. Cecil maneuvered the carriage out of the corner, where Rosie was now sound asleep. After having dessert, she began to drift off, so they'd put her back in the carriage.

"Would you like to go for a stroll now?" he asked, and Hannah looked pleased.

"It's not too dark?" She gazed out the windows to the street outside.

"There's plenty of moonlight, so we should be right." He paid for their food and they were soon on their way. "We don't have to go far. I just thought a bit of fresh air would be nice for a change."

As they strolled along the wooden boardwalk, he snuggled up as close as he could to his wife. "This is nice, don't you think?"

She glanced across at him. "Actually it is," she said. "Tonight has been really lovely, Cecil," she said. "We should have done something like this when Rosie and I arrived."

He didn't say anything, but nodded.

"Things might have been different between us," she said.

He knew she was right.

After wandering around town for about fifteen minutes the air was beginning to get cold. It might be Spring, but the evenings could still be cool. He didn't want the baby or Hannah to get a chill.

When they arrived back home, she changed the baby's diaper while she continued to sleep, and put her down for the night.

"Hannah," he said quietly as she entered the kitchen. She turned to look at him. "Thank you for tonight. I really enjoyed it."

Before she had a chance to answer, he pulled her to him and kissed her. His arms slid up her back and he caressed her. Before long she molded into him and relaxed.

"I really want you, Hannah," he said. "I've been such a fool pushing you away, when this is what I wanted all along."

His fingers reached under her chin and he tipped her head to look up at him. His lips covered hers and her arms came up around his back. Before she had a chance to say anything, he deepened the kiss and was lost to the rest of the world.

Hannah woke up in confusion.

She couldn't work out where she was. Her heart pounded. How did she get here? How could she not know she'd been taken?

She felt an arm snake around her and startled. "It's alright, Hannah." Cecil's gentle words brought it all back.

Last night had been so good. She'd been shocked at first, as she didn't know about these things, but after a short time, she had enjoyed herself.

It was nice to finally be in her husband's bed, and in his arms. She'd had the best sleep she could remember for such a long time. Listening out for Rosie while she slept had left her with only partial rest each night.

But last night was different. She went into a deep sleep and hadn't heard the baby at all.

She suddenly sat up. "Rosie!"

Cecil wrapped an arm around her waist, pulling her back under the covers. "Rosie is fine. I looked in on her a short while ago and she was sleeping soundly." He leaned in and kissed her on the lips. "We have some time before she wakes up."

He wiggled his eyebrows at her.

Rosie began to cry. "Or perhaps not," he said, sounding disappointed.

Hannah sat on the side of the bed and put on her robe. It was a little after dawn, her most favorite time of day. She stretched then stood. "I'll go and change her. Then I'll make breakfast."

By the time she'd changed the baby's diaper and dressed her in dry clothing, Cecil was dressed and had filled the kettle, which was now simmering on the stove.

He had eggs sitting on the side of the counter, and looked ready to make scrambled eggs and bacon. "I thought Rosie could try some scrambled eggs. I've never seen you give it to her," he said. Hannah grabbed an apron and took over.

"I can't wait for the high chair to arrive," she said. "That way she can sit at the table with us. Like a real family."

Cecil looked disappointed at her words. "We *are* a real family." He turned away, and she wondered if he was annoyed.

"I know. That's not what I meant." She stirred the eggs and threw the bacon into a frying pan. "Once Rosie is in a high chair, she can sit at the table with us, like she did at the diner. We'll be able to eat in peace, while she plays."

"Oh. Of course. Sorry."

He toasted the bread while she finished off the main part of the meal, then poured the coffee. "I'm going to start work on the play area before the store opens. I figure the quicker it's done, the sooner we can spend more time together."

"That's a great idea," Hannah said. "I'm sure Rosie is going to love seeing more of her Papa."

As if on cue, Rosie called out. "Papa," she said, reaching her arms out to him. Cecil leaned in to pick her up.

"That's going to be the problem," Hannah told him. "You spoil that child."

He frowned. "No, I don't."

"Yes you do," Hannah said firmly. "You will have to learn restraint in the store, otherwise she'll want to be picked up all the time, and neither of us will get anything done."

He frowned but conceded. "You are right, of course."

They linked hands and bowed their heads in a prayer of thanks for their food. Hannah picked Rosie up off the blanket where she was playing on the floor, and fed her some scrambled egg.

She spat it out. Hannah tried again, and got the same result.

"Put her down and eat your food," Cecil said. "You can try again when you finish your meal."

Hannah did as he asked and Rosie played happily with her toys. "This is why a high chair will be good," she said, then continued eating.

As soon as the meal was over, Cecil headed out to the store. It was still early, but getting a head start had been a priority for him. Hannah was excited for the small play area in the store. It meant she could help Cecil in the way she'd promised before she'd arrived. She would get to spend more time with him, and he would spend more time with Rosie.

The town's people seemed to have warmed to both her and the baby, which was something Hannah had longed for.

She had never felt she belonged anywhere. Even back in Idaho where she'd grown up. From the moment she'd arrived in Grand Falls, she felt like she'd arrived home. The people here were all kind and accepting, even of little Rosie who everyone knew was not a blood relative of either her or Cecil.

It warmed her heart.

She could hear Cecil hammering out in the store. She should go to help she supposed, but needed to tidy the kitchen. Besides, he'd made it abundantly clear this was to be his project, and he wanted to do it his way.

The banging continued, and then she heard Cecil yell. "Blast," he said loudly. She was on the verge of running to the store, but knew he would be displeased if she did. If he was truly injured, he would make his way back to her.

"Papa," Rosie said on hearing his voice.

She looked down at the child playing happily at her feet. "Papa is making you somewhere special to play."

Rosie looked up at her and smiled. "Mama," she said, reaching her little arms up to Hannah. "Mama."

"Oh baby!" her mother said, tears brimming in her eyes.

"Well done, Rosie," Cecil said, entering the kitchen. He held his hand out to his wife. "I have a splinter," he said.

She leaned in and kissed his finger. Not being content with that, he pulled her close and kissed her on the lips. Hannah felt they were finally a family.

Chapter Ten

Everything seemed to happen at once.

The high chair, crib, and stroller all arrived on the train along with the rest of Cecil's monthly order.

The letter Hannah had sent before she'd arrived with Rosie finally arrived too. It had taken far in excess of a month to arrive.

Rosie's play area was well finished, and Cecil was glad he'd decided to make it. Rosie had plenty of space to play in, but the added bonus was she could see Hannah when she was working behind the counter, and of course she could see him too.

The customers loved seeing her too, but because of where he'd built her play area, no one could touch her. He hated to think what it would have been like if he'd made it further out in the store. It made him feel ill.

The bell over the door tinkled and Rosie looked up. She seemed to enjoy seeing customers arrive, and always called out to them.

"Hello!" she called.

Gideon Garrison smiled. "Hello." He turned to Cecil. "Is this your daughter?" the lawyer asked, leaning over the counter to get a better look. "She is very cute."

Cecil's heart thudded. He'd been waiting for news for weeks. Now that he and Hannah were husband and wife in every way, it made perfect sense to make everything official.

"Yes, this is Rosie," he said. "Rosemary."

"I have the paperwork prepared," Gideon said. "It just needs both your signatures."

Cecil leaned in toward him. "It's a surprise for my wife – she doesn't know." He looked about the store. Hannah was nowhere to be seen. "Could we come to your office later today? Say, noon? I'd rather not do this here."

"Are you sure she'll agree? I don't want to waste any more time on this if you think…"

"She'll sign," Cecil interrupted. "She'll be ecstatic, I'm certain."

They shook hands and Gideon left the store. Cecil stared at his back. It was finally happening, and now all he had to do was tell Hannah.

"I don't understand," she said as the three of them headed toward the lawyer's office. "What's it about?"

He just grinned.

The color drained from her face. "You want to end our marriage? Why didn't you…"

"No! Nothing like that." Why would she even think that. They'd been happy together for some time now. An annulment was the last thing he wanted. "It's to do with Rosie."

She went whiter still and stumbled. Hannah looked like she would faint, and he held her around the waist, then backed her onto a nearby bench.

"It was meant to be a surprise," he said. "But I'm going to have to tell you, aren't I?"

She still looked beyond pale. Would she even be able to walk the short distance between here and the lawyer's office?

"I asked Gideon to look into Rosie's status, to ensure there were no family members who could claim her."

Hannah's eyes filled with tears. "We're losing her?" Tears rolled down her face.

Cecil stared at her. "Do you honestly think I would do that to you? To either of us? I love that child, totally adore her. I don't want to give her up."

Hannah swiped the back of her hand across her cheeks. "Then why?"

"Hannah," he said gently, pulling her toward him. "We're adopting her. Rosie is about to become our legal daughter."

Cecil saw now why he should have told her at home. Tears flooded her face, and she snatched Rosie up out of the stroller. She reached for Cecil and they all hugged. "Thank you," she whispered. "But please, next time you do something like this, a little warning would be good."

After she had composed herself, Hannah was ready to move forward.

They continued on their way to the lawyer's office, where they each signed the documentation. Hannah leaned back in her seat, and held Rosie tight.

"Now you are my daughter in every way," she said quietly.

"Mama," Rosie said, and Cecil's heart exploded.

Epilogue

One year later…

The store was busier than it had been for a long time. With the summer months upon them, people were getting out and about more.

Cecil would not complain.

With Hannah laid up, he was struggling to manage the store alone, and had vowed to get help a few hours a day. There were a number of teenagers in town who would rejoice at the opportunity.

There were also some he wouldn't allow anywhere near his store.

The bell over the door tinkled. "Ah, good morning, Mrs Baker," he said pleasantly. Mrs Baker was one of the few people who he really enjoyed seeing.

"Good morning, Mr Delbert," she said. No matter how long they'd known each other, she refused to call him Cecil. On the other hand, she insisted he call her Mrs Baker. "I had a disaster at the diner. My kitchen towels were dropped onto the stove by the help and caught alight."

"My Lord!" Cecil said. "Is everyone alright? Your diner…?"

She put a hand in front of herself to stop him. "Everyone is fine, and the diner is not scarred in anyway. Only my kitchen towels were damaged, and now I must replace them."

He sighed in relief. "That is good to hear," he said, then went out from behind the counter. "They're here, if you'd like to choose your designs."

"Papa, Papa!" Rosie came running into the store on her chubby little legs.

He leaned down and picked her up. "What is it, little one? What has you so excited?"

She leaned into his ear and whispered. "Baby."

He pulled back from her. "Baby?"

"Mama said baby coming."

"Oh!" Still holding Rosie, he ran into the residence. They knew Hannah was close, but he thought they still had some time.

He heard the front door of the Mercantile lock behind him. Mrs Baker thought of everything. She followed him into the residence, and he was grateful for the support.

Hannah lay on the bed, a pile of sheets and towels underneath her. "I'm sorry, Cecil," she said quietly. "My waters broke. There's a mess in the bathroom."

He brushed her concerns away.

"Mama!" Rosie sat on the bed next to her Mama and hugged Hannah tight. "Mama sick?"

"No sweet Rosemary," Mrs Baker said gently. "Mama will be alright. Come to Aunt Edna." She lifted the child and held her tight.

"I'll take Rosemary and get Doc Spencer," she told Cecil. "You put water on to boil and try to stay calm. Keep your wife calm too."

He watched as the pair left the house. "What can I do," he asked as Hannah groaned.

"Put on water, like Mrs Baker said." He put a blanket over her. "I'll be fine, don't fuss," she said. She waved for him to go, but he didn't want to leave her alone.

He knew he had to go. The doctor would be here soon, and he would need boiling water. Cecil went out to the kitchen and filled as many pans with water as he could fit on the stove.

Doc Spencer soon arrived with his medical bag, then sent him packing along with Rosie. "This is no place for a child," he said sternly, sending them out of the house.

"I'll be fine," Hannah said. "I love you," she said, and it broke his heart. Far too many women lost their lives giving birth. He desperately prayed that she wouldn't be one of them.

He leaned down and kissed her. "I love you too," he said, his voice breaking. "More than you'll ever know." He reluctantly left her in the more than capable hands of Doc Spencer.

Mrs Baker stayed behind to help, for which he was very grateful.

He walked the streets with Rosie for what seemed like hours, but was not long at all. Then he went to the diner for coffee, knowing Mrs Baker had staff who would be keeping the place running smoothly. He explained the situation.

He ordered coffee for himself, and a glass of milk for Rosie. He also ordered a muffin for her.

When the coffee arrived he took a sip. It tasted bitter, but he was convinced it was him. There was too much on his mind for him to enjoy his coffee.

Had their baby arrived? Was Hannah alive, or had he lost her giving birth? He couldn't bear the thought of a life without her.

He'd been selfish getting her pregnant. Too many women lost their lives this way – even Rosie's mother had died giving her precious daughter life.

He couldn't continue to sit here doing nothing. He had to get out of here.

Cecil pulled some notes from his pocket and handed it over as they left. He pushed Rosie in the stroller and walked. He had no plan, he just walked.

He soon found himself back at home, wanting to get some sort of update on his wife's progress. As he began to open the door, he heard a heart-wrenching scream, then nothing but silence.

His heart pounded. Had he lost the love of his life?

And then he heard it. The crying of a newborn baby. His baby.

Their baby.

"Papa," Rosie said excitedly. "Baby."

His heart still pounded and he wasn't sure what to do. He didn't want to take Rosie inside due to his deep fear, but he wanted to see his wife. Needed to see for himself if she was alright.

The door suddenly opened wider. "Congratulations, Mr Delbert," Mrs Baker told him. "You have a beautiful baby boy."

He couldn't let himself be joyful until he had the full story. "And what of Hannah? Is my wife…" His voice cracked, and tears filled his eyes. He'd never cried in his adult life before, but he couldn't bear to lose her.

"Hannah is perfectly fine," she said. "The doc needs a few more minutes to clean her up, and then you can both go in to see her."

He stumbled at the news, he was so overwhelmed with joy.

"Cecil, Rosie." It was Hannah's voice and his heart thudded. He didn't think anything could ever sound so wonderful to his ears. "You can come in now."

He pulled Rosie from the stroller and took her into the bedroom to meet her new brother. Her little eyes opened wide, and Cecil got a glimpse of what he probably looked like.

He leaned in and kissed Hannah on the cheek. "Thank you," he whispered.

"Baby." He held Rosie so she could get a better look at her baby brother. She leaned further and kissed his cheek, then kissed her Mama.

"What do you think of Leroy Arthur Delbert? Arthur was Rosie's father's name."

"I think that's perfect." He glanced at Rosie. "Say hello to Leroy."

"Hello Roy," she said, unable to pronounce his name correctly.

"Well, I guess he already has a nickname," Cecil said. "Time to let Mama rest," he told Rosie. He kissed Hannah again, and they left the room.

They went to the sitting room where he picked up his well-worn bible and said a prayer of thanks for bringing his wife safely through this ordeal.

Cecil couldn't imagine his life without his little family. He added another prayer to the Lord for bringing them to him.

The End

From the Author

Thank you so much for reading my book – I hope you enjoyed it.

Cheryl's other books in this series are:

Mail Order Millie
Mail Order Pearl

About the Author

Multi-published, award-winning and bestselling author Cheryl Wright, former secretary, debt collector, account manager, writing coach, and shopping tour hostess, loves reading.

She writes both historical and contemporary western romance, as well as romantic suspense.

She lives in Melbourne, Australia, and is married with two adult children and has six grandchildren. When she's not writing, she can be found in her craft room making greeting cards.

Website: *http://www.cheryl-wright.com/*

Blog: *http://romance-authors.com/*

Facebook Reader Group:
https://www.facebook.com/groups/cherylwrightautho r/